The Life and Times of Lilly the Lash®

Jungle Jive
Written By Julie Woik

To THE Sarasota County Library—

WE NEED TO UNDERSTAND THAT OUR
ACTIONS OFTEN AFFECT OTHERS. IT'S IMPORTANT
THAT WE MAKE OUR CHOICES WISELY!!!

FIND AND KEEP
BALANCE!! YAHOOOOOOOO

J. Woik
MARCH
2016

3 1969 02385 1081

Snow in Sarasota Publishing, Inc.
Osprey, FL 34229
Library of Congress Cataloging in Publication Data
Woik Julie
Jungle Jive
(Book #5 in The Life and Times of Lilly the Lash® series)

p. cm.
ISBN – 978-0-9862979-2-2
1. Fiction, Juvenile 2. Psychology, self-esteem 3. Multi-cultural

First Edition
10 9 8 7 6 5 4 3 2 1

Design: Elsa Kauffman
Illustration: Marc Tobin

Printed by Manatee Printers, Inc., Bradenton, Florida
in the United States of America

ABOUT THIS BOOK

The Life and Times of Lilly the Lash® is a series of fascinating children's books, in which an **EYELASH** teaches life lessons and the importance of strong self-esteem.

Adventurous, yet meaningful storylines told in rhythm and rhyme, accompanied by spectacular cinematic-like illustrations; provide the tomboyish main character with a marvelous opportunity to teach children valuable lessons, while entertaining at every turn.

These whimsical tales for boys and girls age 0 – 10 (to 110!), will break their world of imagination wide open, and transcend their hearts and souls beyond their wildest dreams.

In book five of the series, *Jungle Jive*, Lilly the Lash finds herself in the lush and lavish town of Tree Bark Falls, where a young monkey's idea to generate additional income for the community, is clouded by greed, and quickly turns disastrous. Lilly, only ever seen by the reader, sends in a gentle, nature-loving bear to help the villagers recognize their error in judgment, and provide the guidance needed to restore precious **BALANCE** to their town.

LEARNING ACTIVITIES

Be sure to check out Lilly's website **www.lillythelash.com** to find the array of **FREE** Lesson Plans, Crafting Activities, and Games created for various age ranges and multiple learning levels. These amazing activities are designed for the educational community in a classroom setting, as well as the family structure in a home environment.

Let's use **LOVE** to grow our world!

DEDICATION

To my Dear Friend, my Teacher, my Cheerleader

Although our time together on earth has passed,
your lessons, your love, and your guiding light remain.
I'm so grateful to have had you in my life.

Your memory mends my heart.
My love forever Becky...

JUNGLE JIVE

Book #5 in the Series
The Life and Times of Lilly the Lash®

"Hop, Skip, and Jump!" cried out Teeder the Toad,
"For another 10 times, 'til the end of the road.
We'll strengthen the muscles that help us to play,
And wake up our minds for the start of the day."

Gathering short
of the bank of the brook,
The gang took a rest
to engage in a look.

Suddenly Derek
slid down the mud slope,
Laughing as Hazel
swung out on the rope!

Gliding along with the wind to her back,
Ms. Lilly had sensed she was on the right track.

She could feel the excitement that loomed in the air,
But detected the oncoming cloud of despair.

This jungle was home
to the creatures and such,
Who treasured and cherished
and loved it so much.
"It's obvious, why anyone,
would choose here to live.
The land," noted Lilly,
"has so much to give."

Scoping the scene, she was tickled she'd found,
A way she could parachute onto the ground.
"These seeds," Lilly thought, "are so fluffy and light,
They're sure to provide me an effortless flight."

A plan, that in theory, would certainly work,
But for Lilly the Lash, held an interesting quirk.
The sap of a pine had been cast like a net,
A sticky predicament, she'd not soon forget!

While waiting for Lilly to figure things out,
There's a story I think I should tell you about.
It's a tale that reveals how this sweet clumsy gal,
Had begun as my eyelash, and trustworthy pal.

She had come into being
right out of the blue,
"I'm a gift," she explained,
"made especially for you.
I've been grown from the thoughts
that you hold deep inside,
Those feelings you depend on,
to fill you with pride."

Although I could see...
what she gave me was sight,
Soon my vision became clearer,
more vivid and bright.

"You'll want to take notice," Ms. Lilly would say,

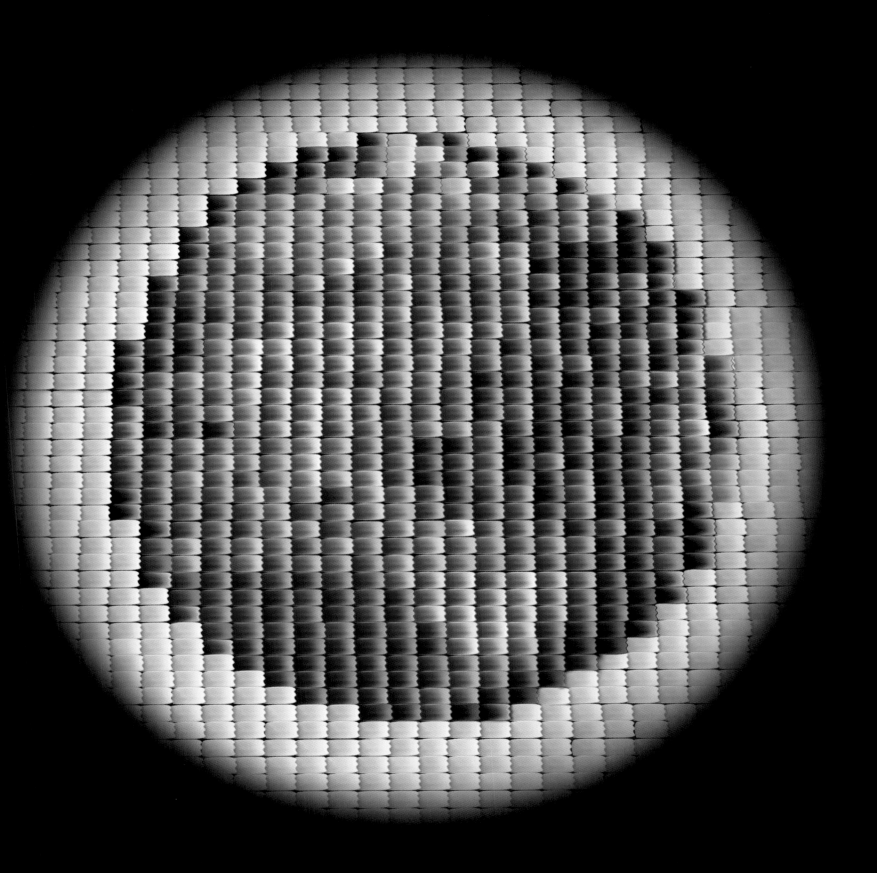

"Of the many encounters that color your day."

We'd stroll on for hours, and not say a word,
But something exceptional always occurred.

It was then that I realized her need to be free,
To give to the world, what she'd given to me.

Lying in bed, drifting off into sleep,
The memories passed by, like the counting of sheep.
My time with Ms. Lilly, was nearing its end,
So I dreamed all the dreams one could dream for a friend.

With bells ringing loudly
through the Town Center halls,
We're summoned to the outskirts,
of Tree Bark Falls.

There, Mother Nature had carved out a space,
"A gem," Lilly envisioned, "I can call my own place."

Peering through the grasses on her way to explore,
Lilly hears a monkey shout, "We could make more!
Selling those trees, to improve Hollow Glade,
Was the easiest money, we could EVER have made!"

"They built their shelter, and we got some loot,
If we advertise to others, they'll all follow suit.
It's easy," swayed Daxton, "and it won't take us long.
We have plenty of trees. What could possibly go wrong?"

The villagers were abuzz, as they went on their way,
   They toyed with the idea, and then gave their okay.
By morning's first light, they were standing in line,
   To take on the duties that Dax had assigned.

Emma and Ella were quick on the draw,
They were sisters, and experts, at handling the saw.
Lexor the Lion used strength from his back,
To pile the large logs on the top of the stack.

Sticks was the tallest, and in charge of the view,
His job was the safety of the rest of the crew.
"Hey Bizzle, can you please move your troops to the side?
Zander's cart," he pointed out, "is exceptionally wide."

As the hours became weeks,
and the weeks became more,
The environment was changing,
looking different than before.

Shade once provided
to Molly B. Mouse,
Was no longer there,
to protect her small house.

The grasses that grew in a variety of greens,
Had been browned by the sun which they hadn't foreseen.
No one considered to think the plan through,
That they may create problems, only time could undo.

Ms. Lilly, disturbed, by the damage being done,
Sat quietly by the water, as for words, she had none.
She needed a way to help open their eyes,
To recognize their actions were both rash and unwise.

It started to sprinkle, then changes came fast,
The storm picked up speed, and brought thunderous blasts.
Dawn would uncover what everyone feared,
That the houses of some, had just **WHOOSH** disappeared.

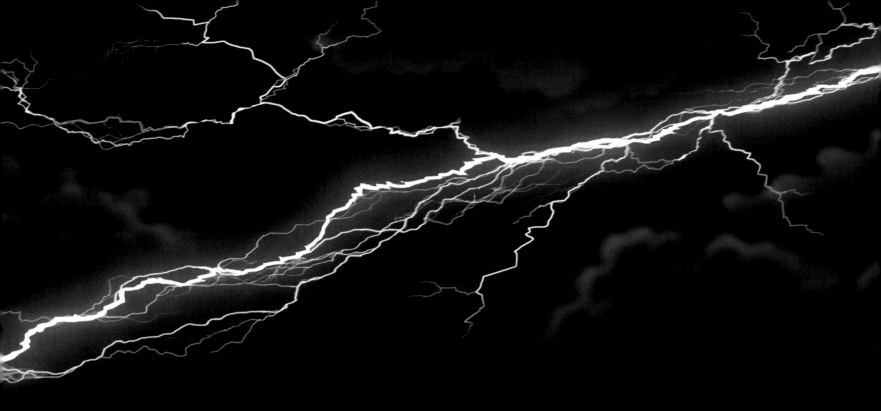

"The lightning, last night, gave our town quite a blow!"
Was the report, Silk the Salamander, gave on his show
"We're lucky we managed to wake and survive,
Stay tuned for live updates, on Radio Jive."

While Lilly the Lash listened close to the news,
She searched for a rock she could work with and use.
Drawing the pictures, by light of the fire,
Added the dimension, and result she desired.

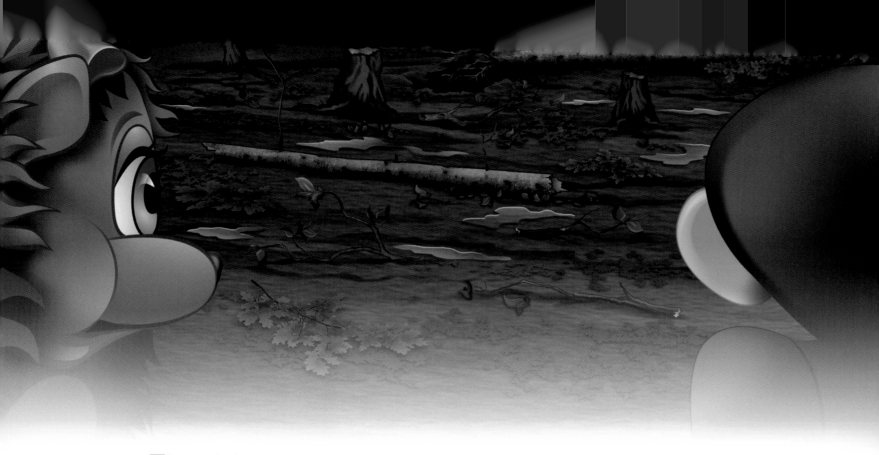

The folks had assembled, to check on the site,
"Oh my dear," whimpered Hazel, "it's truly a fright!"

"Stay calm," Dax reminded the crowd as they stared,
"You'll bunk with your neighbors, while your house is repaired

The uncomfortable silence had surfaced again,
      But was broken, by the arrival, of Old Auntie Bren.
"It's so great to see you," poor Daxton exclaimed,
      "Our city was ravaged, not much has remained."

Scanning around, Auntie Bren was amazed,
That this was the jungle, she applauded and praised,
"You were beautifully shadowed by towering trees,
With vines that performed a ballet in the breeze.

Your hasty decisions have now left you stuck.
Your world is off kilter, and your balance is struck.

Because of your choices, you've reaped what you've sown,
So you'll have to plant saplings, and wait 'til they're grown."

It took them a minute, but then they agreed,
Their behavior was reckless, and their focus was greed.
"It's me. I'm accountable. I'm sorry." Dax said.
"I never even pondered, what might lie ahead."

Lilly had witnessed a wonderful thing,
A promise of hope, that the future would bring.
With her wings fully opened, and the clouds passing by,
Ms. Lilly the Lash, disappeared in the sky.

While spotlighting Daxton, she circled in flight,
To pepper his eye, with a twinkle of light.
The radiating glow, was a positive sign,
That Dax understood, and from here, would be fine.

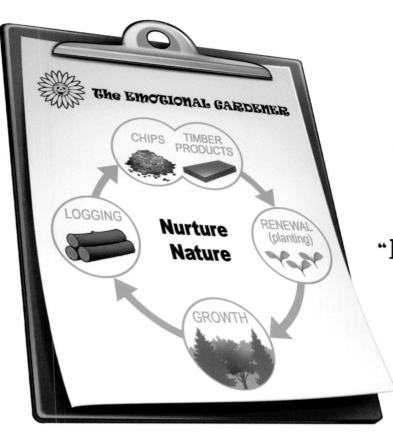

This mystical moment,
was swift to unveil,
How to measure one's options,
and level the scale.
"It'll take us," confirmed Daxton,
"a while to regain,
The refuge, once felt,
by the previous terrain."

Old Auntie Bren moved her truck off the road,
To the middle, where the folks, could begin to unload.
The seedlings and flowers were placed all around,
By the villagers who intended, to rebuild their great town

Sneaking a peek
from the side of the wall,
Ms. Lilly was pleased
she had made the right call.

TREE BARK FALLS

Since everything here,
was now running so smooth.
She could look towards the journey,
that would guide her next move.

The End

. . . are you sure?

FUN FACTS

 Jungles are often thought of as rainforests, but they grow vegetation differently. A rainforest's canopied trees block light, where a jungle has more sunlight reaching the floor, allowing plants to grow abundantly.

 Toads love to eat pesky insects. They've been known to eat 1,000 insects in one day! Toads use their eyes to help them swallow. When they blink, their eyes press into their mouths, moving the food down their throats.

 Hedgehogs rely strongly on their hearing and smell because of their poor eyesight. They like to hang out in thick hedges and under rocks. They communicate through a combination of grunts, snuffles, and squeals. Oooink!

 Bears are very smart! They have superb navigational skills and excellent memories. Their senses are extraordinary when it comes to smell, sight, and hearing; so good, they can smell food from miles away. That's impressive!

 Mice are often thought of as dirty, but actually they are very clean and tidy. They build their burrows with specific areas for storing food and getting sleep. They'll even designate a separate area for their restroom.

 A giraffe's neck is long...but their legs are even longer. This makes their neck too short to reach the ground. As a result, they have to part their front legs or kneel down to get a drink of water. Not an easy task!

 Monkeys use their fingers, toes, and tail to grasp objects, as well as steady themselves on limbs and branches. They love bananas, but many monkeys eat dirt too. (I don't think I'm going to their house for dinner!!)

 Salamanders have tails, but when they're in danger, they'll sacrifice it. The detached tail keeps wriggling to distract the enemy while the salamander escapes. No tail? No problem. They just grow back a new one! Tail-riffic!!!!

 Zebras in a group are called a dazzle. Their stripes form a pattern unique to each animal. When in a large group, the distinct stripes merge into a big mass and make it hard for predators to single out individual animals.

Lilly's hangin' in the Studio
(With real live ART that is!)

The Life and Times of Lilly the Lash®
Art With Heart

A bit tuckered out, having traveled so far,
Ms. Lilly hitched a ride on the bumper of a car.
She relaxed as the stars sparkled bright in the sky,
Then noticed a shooting one, learning to fly.

With the vehicle now slowing, she could see a small light,
It was coming from the alley, to the side on her right.
"I'm not sure," Lilly pondered, "what's happening inside,
As according to the sign, they close daily at five."

Lilly rushed over and peered through the door,
The DESIGN YOUR ART CONTEST was the buzz of the store.
Pibble Dee Pencil was trying to debate,
The value of another, and their gift to create.

(Watch for Book #6 in this Series)

Follow Lilly on her next adventure to
Gallery Gables
Where a pencil learns the important
Life Lesson of
CONFIDENCE

SPECIAL THANKS

To Marc - The Illustrator
Thank you for taking the time and care
to detail and create such beautiful illustrations!
I see how intrigued the children are by your images.
This interest draws them to pick up the book and begin reading.
The initial idea may be entertainment, but the end result is an
IMPORTANT LESSON LEARNED
We're making a difference Marc!!

To Elsa - My Designer
We've been through a lot in the past couple of years.
Life just keeps challenging us...
then strengthening us...and then blessing us!
I'm not sure what's in store, but I know one thing,
I want YOU by my side!!
You in?!

To Paul Beress - Lilly's Hero!
Feeling the urgency for our world to discover Lilly the Lash,
and practice all of her important, essential life lessons,
I asked the universe to provide us with the
guidance, support, and direction needed to move things forward
in a calm, steady, happy, healthy, successful way.
(Since I was asking...I might as well have asked big, right?!!)

Well, Sir, I have to say, you're nothing short of the perfect fit!
You're smart and witty, relaxed and wise, knowledgeable and determined.
Your pace, your tone, and your attitude are exactly what I asked for.
You've brought everything together for Lilly's next step.
We are beyond grateful to have you in our corner.
You're Lilly's Hero! (And mine too!!!)

To Peter Acker - My Photographer
I want to thank you for knowing how to make a person feel comfortable...
and then making them look SPECTACULAR!!!
You're the best!!

To My Mom
You're just so incredible Mom!! One cool cat!!!
I love talking to you every day, and sharing all of the little things in life.
Thank you for loving Dad, and being such a good parent.

Making Our World A Better Place

A percentage of the profit from this book will go to the

MS ™

National Multiple Sclerosis Society

It's fitting that this book focuses on balance.
For the loved ones in my life,
and for those I have yet to have the pleasure of meeting...
let's find a cure.

Let's Restore BALANCE!!